CONTENTS

Cover artwork and illustrations for *Rupert and the Snowbird* by Stuart Trotter
Text and couplets for *Rupert and the Snowbird* by Beth Harwood
Designed by Martin Aggett

We are extremely grateful to John Beck for granting us access to the rare
archive images for *Rupert at School*, from his personal collection.

*This Book
Belongs To*

. . . .

. . . .

Endpapers and contents page adapted from the *Rupert Annual*, 1958, illustrated by Alfred Bestall

THE 75TH RUPERT ANNUAL

CELEBRATING
90
1920 - 2010

EXPRESS NEWSPAPERS

EGMONT
We bring stories to life

Published in Great Britain 2010 by Egmont UK Limited
239 Kensington High Street, London W8 6SA
Rupert Bear™: © 2010 Classic Media Distribution Limited/Express Newspapers.
All Rights Reserved.

ISBN 978 1 4052 5239 3
Printed in Italy

All rights reserved. No part of this publication may be reproduced, stored in a retrieval
system or transmitted, in any form or by any means, mechanical, photocopying, recording
or otherwise, without the prior permission of the publisher and copyright holder.

No. 75

£7.99

★ FROM TOURTEL TO TROTTER

✦ 90 Years of Rupert Bear

Who would have thought, when a little bear in checked trousers first appeared in the *Daily Express*, that ninety years later Rupert Bear would still be a household name?

Rupert as we know him now – resplendent in his red pullover and yellow and black checked scarf and trousers – looked a little different when Mary Tourtel first drew him in 1920, later painting him in a blue pullover. But that little bear had the same passion for adventure that has led him into peril many a time over the last nine decades, and has gained him countless friends in the process.

The world that Mary Tourtel created for Rupert bore only a slight resemblance to the world at the time. Rupert's adventures took him out of cosy Nutwood and into a fairy-tale land full of nursery characters, wily creatures and medieval monarchs whom Rupert would either befriend or have to escape from in a most elaborate fashion.

The first story reproduced in this annual, *Rupert at School*, however, shows Rupert in a more familiar scenario – standing up to the school bullies and proving the strength of his stalwart friendships with Edward Trunk and Bill Badger. Tourtel's story was first published in the *Daily Express* in 1933.

Mary Tourtel was the wife of Herbert Bird Tourtel, the deputy editor of the *Daily Express*, and she was already an established illustrator when she

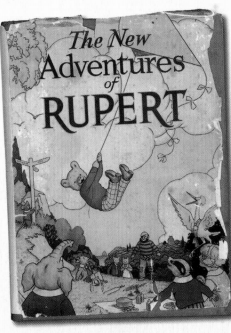

was appointed to create a new feature for children on the newspaper's women's page. She had illustrated two previous series for the paper: 'When Animals Work' and 'In Bobtail Land'; the latter featuring a rabbit whose adventures were not dissimilar to those of Rupert in later years.

Tourtel drew Rupert for fifteen years, until the mid-1930s, when she felt she could no longer work. Stanley Marshall, then the children's editor of the *Daily Express*, needed to find a replacement – and hired Alfred Bestall to assist Tourtel.

Bestall was credited with creating the Rupert we now most commonly recognise, in his signature red-and-yellow ensemble. Bestall was a skilled illustrator whose previous work had included advertisements for the London Underground, and satirical cartoons for society magazines such as *Tatler*.

In 1936 the first-ever Rupert Annual was published, entitled *The New Adventures of Rupert*, promising '... lots of fun inside'. Five Rupert stories featured in the annual, stories that had been featured sequentially in the newspaper in the previous year.

Out of respect for Mary Tourtel, Bestall did not sign his illustrations of Rupert until after Tourtel's death in 1948, though Bestall's illustrative style is beautifully distinct.

In contrast to the rule to which Tourtel adhered, that there was to be no magic in

Rupert stories, Bestall took Rupert on magical adventures, in which he met many strange creatures.

Rupert's Queer Path, originally published in the *Daily Express* in 1949 and first reproduced in the 1951 annual, is one such adventure. Rupert's friend Tigerlily casts a spell over the Bears' new crazy paving, and the path sends Rupert and Bill into Crazy Land, where frogs talk, birds don't fly and trees grow upside down.

Another popular element that Bestall introduced was origami. Rupert Annuals featured a 'how to make' section in which Bestall explained how to fashion a ball, a glider or an elephant out of a single sheet of paper. You can find some of Bestall's origami activities reproduced in this annual in tribute, alongside puzzles chosen especially from the Rupert Bear archives.

Alfred Bestall illustrated Rupert Bear for thirty years before he took the decision to retire, though he worked sporadically on Rupert stories up until the 1970s. In the period after Alfred Bestall's retirement, as a suitable long-term artist was sought, a small group of illustrators, including Alex Cubie, worked on Rupert.

Eventually John Harrold took on the mantle full-time in 1978, at first painting the titles and endpapers for the annuals. Harrold's first forays into illustrating Rupert had come five years

before, when he illustrated a recipe book for Collins – *Lots of Fun to Cook with Rupert Bear* – so he was already adept in representing the little bear on paper. Harrold's contribution to the look of the Rupert annuals was significant; he designed the L-shaped illustrations on the stories' title pages. John Harrold and writer Ian Robinson also created the Sage of Um and his flying upside-down Brella, one of a fleet of peculiar objects to fly over Nutwood. In *Rupert and the Birthday Adventure*, Rupert, Bill Badger and Bill's little cousin Bea take a flight in a hot-air balloon to the oft-visited Kingdom of the Birds – and inadvertently win a balloon race!

Each of Rupert's illustrators has embellished Rupert's world, and given the little bear a wide and varied circle of friends that still includes Bill Badger and Edward Trunk. Stuart Trotter is no exception. In becoming the official illustrator of Rupert Bear in 2008, he continued a tradition that was now over eighty years old, and refreshed Rupert for a new generation of readers.

For this special anniversary annual, Trotter has devised and illustrated a brand-new Rupert story entitled *Rupert and the Snowbird*, a tale that sits neatly in the canon of classic Rupert stories, and embodies the traditional values of bygone days.

We hope you enjoy this, the 75th Rupert Annual, and please join us in wishing Rupert Bear a very happy 90th birthday!

Illustration by Mary Tourtel on the
cover of *Monster Rupert*, 1932

Cover image courtesy of John Beck

Illustrated by MARY TOURTEL

Originally published in the *Daily Express* in 1933

No. 1—School Begins Again

Christmas holidays are over now, and school begins today.
Bill and Edward call for Little Bear as they pass by that way.
Rupert's ready for them, he has packed his satchel overnight,
Looked up his pencils, pens and books, so that everything's all right.

No. 2—Preparing for Battle

Still yet the snow lay on the fields, though all the roads were clear.
The snow was banked on either side, so, when they to school drew near,
They prepare to have some fun; they made of snowballs quite a lot,
Ready for a battle with the boys, and to get in their first shot.

Rupert at School

No. 3—Hippo the Bully

No sooner had they stepped inside the schoolyard than they see
Hubert Hippo, and the Twins with him, looking frightened as can be.
Now Hubert Hippo loved to tease and bully anyone
Smaller than himself, and hurt them too; he thought this rather fun.
He seized Reggie's arm and twisted it, till Reggie yelled with pain.
Taking careful aim, said Rupert, "Look! He's at his tricks again."

No. 4—A Well-Landed One

The snowball landed fair and true right on to Hippo's ear;
Being nice and hard, it gave a sting, and Hippo yelped with fear.
Quickly he was bombarded by the rest the others threw;
The Twins, they do not wait to see what happened, off they flew,
Rejoiced indeed to get away from that big bully there.
They did not see 'twas Edward Trunk, and Bill, and Little Bear.

No. 5—Trooping into School

Just then the bell rings; into school the scholars there all troop,
But Edward keeps a watchful eye on a certain little group.
Wally Wolf, and Hippo, and that sly Reynard Fox, they're all great
friends,
Who work together, bully, cheat, to gain their unfair ends.
Reggie and Rex are glad indeed to be with Little Bear.
And big Edward Trunk, well they know they're safe from Hippo there.

No. 6—Reynard on Mischief Bent

There's a new master for their form this term. Some think that he
Looks easy game; to play a trick on him these boys agree.
So when the master's back was turned, and he was all intent
On showing Rupert what was wrong, Reynard Fox on mischief bent
Crept out; no least sound did he make, when a piece of string he tied
To the blackboard's easel; quickly then back to his seat he hied.

Rupert at School

No. 7—Reynard Tricks the New Master

Reynard, from where he sat, could pull the string, soon came a clatter;
Down fell the easel, blackboard too. "Good gracious! What's the matter?"
Exclaimed the master, turning round, and then a grin he caught
On Bill's face. "That's the culprit there," of course at once he thought.
Wily Reynard Fox had thrown the string down by the side of Bill,
Where it caught the master's eye, and thus he was convinced more still.

No. 8—Bill Gets the Blame

The master was very angry now; "So you thought this trick to play,"
Said he to Bill, "because I'm new and this is my first day.
But you don't know me: you will find you've made a great mistake,
For punishment you shall stay in, when the rest go out for break."

No. 9—Rupert is Angry with Reynard

"What happened, Bill?" asked Little Bear, when all had gone to play
At break. "It was that Reynard Fox," said Bill. "You know his way.
He tied that string. What could I do?" Of course they knew quite well,
That e'en against that sneaky Fox, tales they must never tell.
But Rupert's angry for his friend. Said he: "It is a shame!
He's just a sneak, that Reynard Fox, to let you take the blame.
It isn't fair. I'm going now to give him of my mind."
And off went Rupert in hot haste that Reynard Fox to find.

No. 10—Rupert Speaks his Mind

There in the playground Rupert saw, together were the three,
Hipp and Reynard Fox. Going up to them said he:
"A pretty lot you are, I think. You never play the game,
But cheat and bully. Reynard Fox, you know it is a shame
To let Bill in for punishment, a nasty trick you played."
But they only laughed and jeered — they're three, so of him they're not afraid.
Just then the bell began to clang. It is the end of break,
And all must go back into school, no further words they spake.

Rupert at School

No. 11—Underhand Work

It was some days later, and the hour when Rupert's class was due
To give their exercises in for correction, as they knew.
Bill goes to his desk to get his work when, "Oh," cried he, "my books!
They are just covered all with blots." At once then Rupert looks
Inside his desk. Alas he finds the same, to his surprise,
For on opening his books he sees big blobs of ink; he cries:
"Mine, too, are inked. Someone's done this!" "Oh!" calls Edward in distress,
"My exercises! All are spoilt." Who's done this they can guess.

No. 12—Called Up

The master does not know the boys; he's not been long there yet.
So when he found their books all inked, then angry did he get.
He thought them careless; called them up, thrust the book at Little Bear,
"Disgraceful!" said he, "work like this to send me, sir, you dare.
And you, Trunk and Badger, both as bad. I'll teach you not to shirk;
You will be caned, the three of you, for this untidy work."

No. 13—They Make a Plan

As Rupert, Bill and Edward Trunk walked home from school that day,
They made a vow they'd find the one who on them that trick did play.
So they planned to go next day to school, in good time, then to hide
In their classroom, so they can watch, to see what will betide.

No. 14— The Culprit Discovered

Early next day they get to school. To Edward's dire dismay
There is no hiding place for him, he's too big, so he must stay
Outside; he fears he'll miss some fun; they tell him to wait about,
Ready to dash inside at once he hears them give a shout.
Rupert and Bill then hide beneath the master's desk, and wait.
Soon they hear someone tiptoe in, and to Rupert's desk go straight.
They both peep out; 'tis as they thought; the culprit they see there,
Is Wally Wolf, and searching through the books of Little Bear.

No. 15—Caught in the Act

"Ha, ha! We've caught you in the act. We thought that it was you,"
Calls Rupert, dashing out at him. Bill follows closely too.
Wally gives a yelp, he drops the book as though it were red hot.
Then with one frightened glance at them he dashes from the spot.

No. 16—No Escape for Wally

But Rupert had him in his grip. He held on to him tight,
And shouted, "Edward! Come in, quick, we've caught the one all right."
In dashed Edward just in time. "Help! Let go!" Wally cried.
But the three seized hold of arms and legs and carried him outside.

No. 17— The Master's Suspicions about Wally

Now their master happened to have heard angry voices and the din,
And someone shout: "We've caught the one." He decided to step in.
A glimpse he had of all the three, as they were carrying out
Wally Wolf. Thinks he: "Some trick he's played on them, I have no doubt."
The open desk next caught his eye, and lying on the ground
Was Rupert's book, work neatly done, and no blots there he found.
Then came the thought into his mind, had they caught Wally there
About to tamper with their books, and those of Little Bear?

No. 18—A Ducking for Wally

Holding Wally by his legs and arms, they carry him to where
A pump stands in the stable yard, with a tub beneath it there.
"No, no!" yelps Wally, when he sees what they intend to do;
"Let me go. I'll never ink your books again, I promise you."
But they only laugh; then with a will they lift him up; "Oh, stop!"
He yells; then leaving go their hold, they let him fall in plop.

Rupert at School

No. 19—Wally Goes Off Whimpering

Oh, what a soaking Wally had before they let him go,
All dripping wet; a picture he of damp and sniffling woe.
"Perhaps you'll leave our books alone for the future," called out Bill.
"You'll be sorry for this," Wally cried; "I'll tell my dad, I will.
He'll see you're punished." Then they laughed. In sobs and tears he went,
He, who others often bullied sore, their treatment did resent.

No. 20—Wally Tells the Master

Wally, thirsting for revenge, by chance just then the master met.
"Why, what has happened, Wolf?" he said, when he saw him dripping wet.
"Oh, sir," said Wally, cringing there, "those three, they tried to drown
Me in the tub – Bear, Badger, Trunk." Said the master, with a frown,
"What were you doing at their desks? Perhaps you will explain."
Wally stood there nonplussed. Did he know? Then the master spoke again:
"And you come telling tales to me. Enough I saw and heard
To know that you were in the wrong. You got what you deserved."

No. 21—At Play

For the time being after that, young Wally and his crew
Left Rupert and his friends alone, 'twas wiser so to do.
Not one of them was popular with any of the boys,
They never joined them in their games, or sports, or other joys.
Though secretly they're envious when they see Little Bear
Playing in the games with his chums, they go by nose in air.

No. 22— Rupert Works with a Will

So passed the weeks; and Rupert worked at lessons with a will,
For he'd made a promise to his dad that he wanted to fulfil,
To work hard all the term, and ne'er let his attention stray,
For if he does well, Daddy said, when comes next holiday,
He'll take him, and his mummy too, with a little friend maybe,
To spend three weeks at that jolly place called Winkleton-on-Sea.

RUPERT'S SHORT CUT

"I say, you chaps," says Rupert, "I've just found a short cut up to the windmill." "Don't tell us," cries Bill, "let Algy and me try to find it for ourselves!" "Right-o, be off with you," says Rupert. "Only remember this: you mustn't get in the river and there must be no breaking through any hedges. The gates are all open, but Farmer Wurzel says that nobody must set foot in any field that contains a red board." Algy scampers down and over a bridge, but Bill decides not to cross the water. Which of them finds the short cut?

Answer on page 68.

Illustrated by ALFRED BESTALL

RUPERT'S QUEER PATH

Because Tigerlily used magic
on the path, Rupert and Bill
had to visit Crazy Land.

Originally published in the *Daily Express* in 1949

RUPERT GETS AN IDEA

"That ground is damp," says Mr Bear,
"And nothing seems to grow well there."

So Rupert wants to find a plan,
To make it better, if he can.

"Let's make a crazy path!" he cries,
And Mr Bear thinks this is wise.

Next day they both go out to choose
The stone and sand that they will use.

Rupert and his father have been working very hard trying to straighten a neglected corner of their garden. When they pause for a rest Mr Bear looks very thoughtful. "Do you know," he says, "I've always had difficulty with this spot. It's dark and it's gloomy and it needs changing somehow. Have you any ideas?" "I can get some if I think hard," smiles Rupert. At length, Rupert and his father decide they have done enough for the day and stroll towards the cottage where Mrs Bear meets them.

Rupert settles down to a jigsaw puzzle, but he can't get his mind off that garden problem, and suddenly he jumps up. "I've got an idea," he says. "We must change the path so that we don't get our feet muddy. Can't we put down some slabs and make it a crazy paving?" After breakfast they catch the first bus into the nearest town and soon they are looking around a big yard filled with rocks, stone, poles and heaps of sand. Mr Bear chooses the slabs he needs, not too heavy, not too thin, and some sand.

RUPERT MAKES A PROMISE

When Tigerlily sees it come,
She closely questions her dear chum.

The Chinese girl says, "That is fun;
Please let me know when it is done."

Now Mr Bear and Rupert too
Have lots and lots of work to do.

At last the path is quite complete,
No more will they have muddy feet.

Rupert notices his friend, Tigerlily, and she runs over. "Lorry bring stone. You going to build new house?" asks the little Chinese girl. "No," laughs Rupert. "We're only putting down some crazy paving." "You making crazy path," Tigerlily cries. "You tell me when path is finished, yes please." "Why, of course you can see it when it is done," says Rupert. "But why not come and help us make it?" The little girl is quiet for a moment. "No, that not do," she says. "Me only come when finish."

For some days they work and Rupert takes great care to see that the paving is level, but he can't get the strange request of the Chinese girl out of his mind. "Why did the idea of the crazy paving make her so excited?" he thinks. At length the slow job is finished and Mr Bear looks with pride at his work. "That was a jolly good idea of yours, Rupert," he says. "Our feet will never get muddy here again." All at once there is a sound of someone running, and Bill Badger appears.

RUPERT KEEPS HIS PROMISE

Then Bill and Rupert quickly go,
To let young Tigerlily know.

"The path is nice and flat," says she,
"But much more crazy it should be."

The Chinese girl says, "I know how
To make it crazy for you now."

She takes a wand and powder out,
And starts to sprinkle it about.

"When the slabs arrived the Chinese girl, Tigerlily, was watching," Rupert tells Bill. "For some reason she was very excited and she made me promise to tell her when the path was finished. Come on. We'll go now." They race over the Common until the conjurer's curious house appears and they meet their pal carrying a black bag. "You path finish?" asks Tigerlily. "That's good. Me come quick." The three friends hurry back to Mr Bear's garden and Rupert runs on to the new path.

"Oh, please," begs Rupert, "do tell us if there is any way of making the path better." The little girl smiles mysteriously. "Very well," she says. "You want real crazy path. I give you one. You come and watch." First she makes them stand at the edge of the bushes. "Nobody must stand on the path while me working," she says. "Now watch." From her black bag, she takes a wand and a small box. Then she sprinkles powder on some of the slabs and waves her wand while she murmurs queer Chinese words.

RUPERT GETS A SHOCK

But when they reach the last big stone,
It splits in half, all on its own.

Now Tigerlily is afraid,
A really crazy path she's made.

When Rupert's father comes along,
He wants to know what has gone wrong.

"It looks all right," says Mr Bear,
Then water squirts into the air.

They move closer and gaze more intently as the little girl reaches the last slab on the path. Suddenly, with a great crack, the stone splits right across. Tigerlily starts in consternation and, hurrying Rupert and Bill away from the paving, she stares wildly at her wand. "Oh dear! Me not mean to do that," she cries. "Me been too clever this time." "But, please, what have you done?" asks Rupert. "The path looks just the same as before." "No, it not the same," sobs Tigerlily. "It really crazy path now."

Just then Mr Bear saunters up. "Your friend is in a great hurry," he says. "What's the matter?" "She saw our lovely new paving and said it wasn't crazy enough," says Rupert. Back in the garden Mr Bear looks closely at the path. "It looks quite all right except that Tigerlily has been putting some powder on the stones," he says. He moves to walk on the path, but the moment he treads on the first slab a jet of water shoots upwards and splashes him all over. Rupert is almost too astonished to speak.

RUPERT RUNS TO HELP BILL

Poor Mr Bear is cross indeed,
And rushes off at such great speed.

Bill wants to tread upon the stone,
Though Rupert says, "Leave well alone."

But when Bill goes to try his luck,
He quickly finds his feet are stuck.

The only thing that Bill can do,
Is wriggle each foot from its shoe.

Mr Bear is very much annoyed. "That wretched girl has put some of the conjurer's magic into my beautiful new path," he storms. "I'll go straight to her father." Rupert gazes anxiously after him, but his pal grins mischievously. "We'd better keep off that path until Daddy gets back," says Rupert, clutching at Bill's arm and trying to hold him back. But Bill insists. "Didn't you notice what Tigerlily did?" he smiles. "She only put powder and magic on some of the stones."

Bill tells Rupert his new idea for a game. "Don't you see?" he cries. "We both saw which of the slabs got the magic. Let's see if we can walk right across the path on the other slabs." And he starts along the path, carefully missing the one on which Mr Bear trod. Next minute he has stopped and is clutching his foot. "Hi! What's wrong?" asks Rupert. Bill is still tugging at his shoes. "I can't move them," he pants. "My feet are stuck fast." Edging past the bushes Rupert hurries to his side.

RUPERT TAKES A SLIDE

The shoes are stuck so firmly there,
"Oh, this is dreadful!" says the bear.

When Rupert thinks that he will go,
He starts to shake from head to toe.

He jumps away all on his own,
But lands upon the broken stone.

Before the bear can step aside,
He falls straight down a rocky slide.

The two pals kneel at the edge of the path and gaze at Bill's shoes. "There, that must be the special magic of that slab," says Rupert. "Whoever treads on it gets stuck there. We'll never get those shoes back until Tigerlily returns." Bill frowns. "I'll not be beaten," he says. "I'm going to finish my game." "No," cries Rupert. "You mustn't go another step on this path without your shoes." Rupert sees that the only way to keep him quiet is to go along the path himself, so he steps slowly and his pal watches.

Near the end he gives a terrific leap and tries to get clear, but he jumps short and lands on the last slab which Tigerlily has cracked. To his horror the two halves fold downwards under his weight. The strange behaviour of the last slab has taken Rupert more by surprise than any of the others. He hears Bill's voice round the bend asking what he is doing, but before he can save himself he has dropped between the two halves of the slab and is sliding down a steep and very slippery chute.

RUPERT IN CRAZY LAND

Though Rupert has a nasty fall,
He finds he isn't hurt at all.

A great, fat frog tells Rupert now,
"You've come to Crazy Land, somehow."

When Rupert tries to walk along,
His feet are taking him quite wrong.

Large flowers are growing in a cave,
They look at him and then they wave.

Rupert's rush through the tunnel is brought to a sudden stop and he finds himself in a bright cave. He gazes for some minutes at a sign above his head. "Why, I do believe I can read that," he thinks. "It says 'Welcome'. But why is it upside-down? Oh dear, where am I?" he murmurs. A deep voice near his ear makes him start violently. On a shelf in the rock is a huge frog-like creature. "You want to know where you are, do you?" says the frog. "Why don't you use your brain? This is Crazy Land, of course."

Rupert is very startled. "I know I was on the crazy path but I didn't want to come here," he says. "I want to go back home but something has happened to my feet and I can't move forward." "If you want to move forward all you have to do is to try and move the other way," says the frog. Feeling quite bewildered, Rupert tries to press his back against the wall of the rock and he finds that he is moving steadily forward. There are lots of passages and caves all brightly lit, though no light can be seen.

RUPERT IS JOINED BY BILL

Now Rupert finds he's back once more,
Inside the cave he left before.

As Rupert wonders what to do,
Poor Bill comes tumbling downwards too.

"Oh dear," gasps Bill, "I've had a fright";
But otherwise he is all right.

So Rupert starts to show his chum,
This crazy place to which they've come.

After a while Rupert goes faster but, reaching a large cave, he stops and stares. "This is idiotic," he says. "Surely I'm back where I started." "Of course you are," grumbles the frog. "I tell you this is Crazy Land. As long as you try to get out, you'll always come back here. Why don't you try to walk farther into the cave?" Rupert is beginning to feel exasperated. He hears a sudden click and a little swishing noise and the next instant a figure rushes down the chute. "Why, it's Bill!" shouts Rupert.

The little bear helps his pal to get up. "Is that you, Rupert?" whispers Bill, shakily. "No, I'm not hurt. But where are we? I called to you when you went round the bend, but you didn't answer, so I followed and when I trod on the last big slab this happened." Rupert tells Bill all that he has learnt about the Crazy Land. "Look, there's the crazy frog who'll explain everything to you," he begins. Then he gives a start, for the shelf in the rock is quite empty.

RUPERT MEETS STRANGE BIRDS

By walking backwards soon they find,
That they have left the caves behind.

"Just look at that," cries Rupert Bear,
"That tree has roots up in the air."

The strangest birds come flocking round,
They walk and never leave the ground.

The crazy frog comes into sight,
And all the birds depart in fright.

"It's not nice to be left alone in this place," says Rupert. "However, I must try and get out." So they try to back into the cave and almost at once they find themselves gazing out into misty daylight. Walking out of the cave the two friends see that they are in a wide space surrounded by high cliffs which are half hidden in mist. "I know, let's climb right up that tree," says Bill. Rupert agrees, but as they move forward, the tree slowly and silently turns and stands with its roots in the air.

Before they know what is happening they are surrounded by dozens of birds which have walked up from all directions and stare at the two pals inquisitively. "What do they want?" says Rupert. "Why are they so quiet?" The queer-shaped birds crowd in closer and closer, but just as the pals are getting really worried, they all seem to take fright and scuttle away at top speed. "Whatever can have made them do that?" breathes Bill in relief. "Look!" cries Rupert. "Up there, above your head!"

RUPERT LEARNS TO FLY

The frog then tells them something queer,
"Except the birds, we all fly here."

"What nonsense!" says the little bear,
But then the frog flies in the air.

"I think I'll try it," Rupert cries,
And up he goes, to his surprise.

When Bill sees what his chum can do,
He calls, "I'm coming up with you!"

Rupert is so relieved to see the frog that he pours out his questions. "Steady on," says the frog, "one question at a time. Birds are the only creatures here that can't fly. Everyone else can!" At the frog's words Rupert sighs. "What nonsense you do talk," he says. The frog looks bored and sighs even more deeply. "You get duller and duller," he croaks. "Look!" He takes a deep breath and spreads out his four legs, and next moment he is floating above their heads.

The crazy frog glides smoothly through the mist for a while and then settles near the two pals. "D'you mean that anyone can do it?" cries Rupert. "Why, it's all too easy," says the frog. "Just spread your arms and think about flying and there you are." Feeling quite bewildered Rupert does as he is told, and to his delight he feels his feet leaving the ground. Rupert is thrilled at his new adventure. "Wait for me," cries Bill. "I must try this. Is it really easy?"

RUPERT FLIES WITH BILL

They stop to rest and try to find
A way to leave this place behind.

To reach the cliff top would be best,
But soon they need a place to rest.

Just then a kitten passes by,
And asks them how they like to fly.

"Go through that tunnel," says the cat,
"You may get home, if you do that."

Rupert and Bill practise all the tricks of flying and, at length, their arms get tired and they glide back to the rocks. All at once Rupert leans forward. "I've got an idea," he says. "Now if we can fly, we can take ourselves over those cliffs and back to Nutwood. If we get tired we can just float around for a rest." When they have had a rest the two pals take off and fly upwards. "I say," gasps Bill, "do you think we have any chance of reaching Nutwood?"

Rupert and Bill are just thinking of going down when they see an enormous kitten. "Lovely day for flying, isn't it? You're strangers, aren't you?" says the kitty. "We've never flown before," says Rupert wearily, "and we're trying to get back to Nutwood." The two friends, seeing a shelf near them, land and spread out in relief. "Whew, I wish we were safe back home," sighs Bill. The crazy kitten hears them and comes back. "There's a tunnel behind you. Try that," smiles the kitten.

RUPERT FINDS A TRAPDOOR

Now Rupert walks too near the edge,
And topples backwards from the ledge.

But Rupert saves himself all right,
And soon comes flying into sight.

A blaze of light ahead they see,
And wonder now where they can be.

They're in a cave as bright as day,
A trapdoor tells them, "keep away".

As the kitten fades into the mist the two pals gaze after it. Behind them is the tunnel. Rupert starts, but the moment he tries to take a step forward he finds himself toppling back into the mist. For a time Bill hears and sees nothing. Then, to his intense relief, Rupert appears flying through the mist. "Mind you don't make the same mistake that I did," calls the little bear, as he floats into the tunnel. "You're still in Crazy Land, so if you want to walk forward you must try and walk backwards."

Bill soon catches Rupert up in spite of the darkness. "This is a queer place," he says. "These rocks don't hurt my feet half as much as they would at home." Feeling their way along, they become used to the gloom, until, rounding a corner, they see a blaze of light ahead. Creeping forward, Rupert and Bill reach the end of the tunnel. "It's as bright as it was in the first cave," says Bill. "Where does the light come from?" Glancing upwards he gives a shout. "Look, there's a trapdoor."

RUPERT TELLS THE CONJURER

A sudden gust of wind now comes,
And through the door it blows the chums.

Now Rupert is relieved to find,
The Crazy Land is left behind.

The Chinese conjurer is there,
He's talking now to Mr Bear.

The chums explain where they have been,
And all the crazy things they've seen.

The minute they try to move backwards the trapdoor opens, and a sudden, tremendous wind whirls them out of the cave and straight up into the brighter light above. As soon as the two friends are out of the cave, the trapdoor closes quickly and silently. "This looks like a real room," says Rupert, in great relief. "I do believe we are out of Crazy Land at last." He listens intently. "Yes," he breathes excitedly. "There's someone talking beyond that curtain and I know whose voice it is."

Rupert and Bill both listen carefully. "You're right," whispers Bill. "I know that voice, too. It's your daddy." They creep forward and peer through the curtain. Sure enough, Mr Bear is there and is telling about the queer things that have happened to his new path while the conjurer stands frowning and looking very grave and thoughtful. On catching sight of Rupert and Bill the two grown-ups are very startled, and the little bear pours out the story of his extraordinary adventure.

RUPERT GETS BILL A CARRIAGE

The conjurer looks most severe,
He says, "I think my girl is here."

Poor Tigerlily is so sad,
Her father thinks she's very bad.

"These stones do hurt my feet," says Bill.
"It really makes me feel quite ill."

They go, at once, the path to see,
And Bill is wheeled quite easily.

The conjurer declares that he has seen Tigerlily return, so the little party move off towards the house in the gardens. Sure enough, the little girl is there. The wand and her black bag are on the ground and she is turning the pages of a heavy Chinese book. As Rupert runs to her she starts anxiously. "Why you come?" she asks. "You in trouble with the crazy path, no?" When her father arrives he bids her to get up. Then the conjurer lifts the wand and they hear him talking gravely in Chinese.

In a few minutes the conjurer returns to the little group. "Me punish Tigerlily," he says. "But not yet. Your crazy path very serious. Come, we go back and put it right, and take away magic." Bill is hobbling painfully in the rear. The conjurer is stopped by the crying of Bill who does not want to be left behind. "No can wait," cries the conjurer. "If Bill no walk he must ride. We lend little carriage." So Tigerlily runs to fetch a garden basket, and soon the whole party is hurrying across the Common.

RUPERT GREETS HIS MOTHER

The conjurer now takes his flask,
To start upon his urgent task

With magic oil he works so well,
That very soon he breaks the spell.

"I'm glad that's done!" says Mr Bear,
"It was a very strange affair."

Now Mrs Bear comes on the scene,
In time to hear where they have been.

The conjurer stares earnestly and he makes Tigerlily tell him which places she has treated with her magic. After that, he bends over each stone muttering some strange Chinese words and letting fall a tiny drop of oil from his flask. The conjurer works slowly and carefully, going from stone to stone. "Now it is all done," he declares. "No more magic in the new path. No more trouble." He stands on the great cracked slab which had let Rupert and Bill into Crazy Land and shows them that all is well.

But Rupert is worried. "He said he was going to punish Tigerlily," he murmurs. "I hope he won't be too hard on her." After watching the conjurer and Tigerlily out of sight Rupert runs back and finds his mother standing on the crazy path. "I came to see what was happening," she says. "This is the first time I've seen your new path." Rupert laughs gleefully. "It's lucky that you weren't here before!" he cries. "You would have dropped through right into Crazy Land just as Bill and I did!"

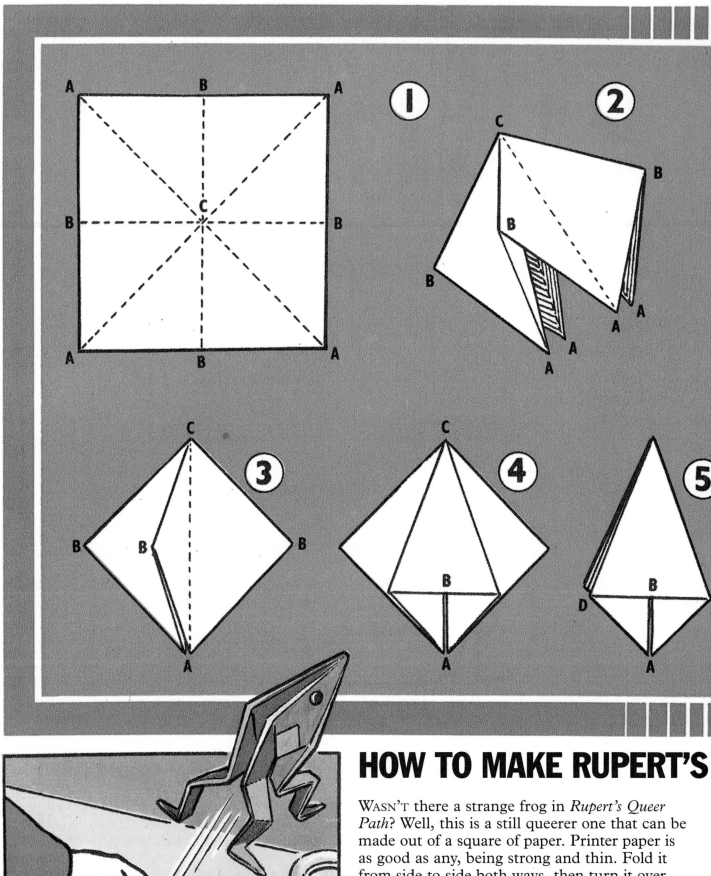

HOW TO MAKE RUPERT'S

WASN'T there a strange frog in *Rupert's Queer Path*? Well, this is a still queerer one that can be made out of a square of paper. Printer paper is as good as any, being strong and thin. Fold it from side to side both ways, then turn it over and fold opposite corners together so that the creases look like Figure 1. Next bring the points marked A together, leaving the four B's sticking out (Figures 2 and 3). Open the fold at one of the points marked B and carefully press it flat,

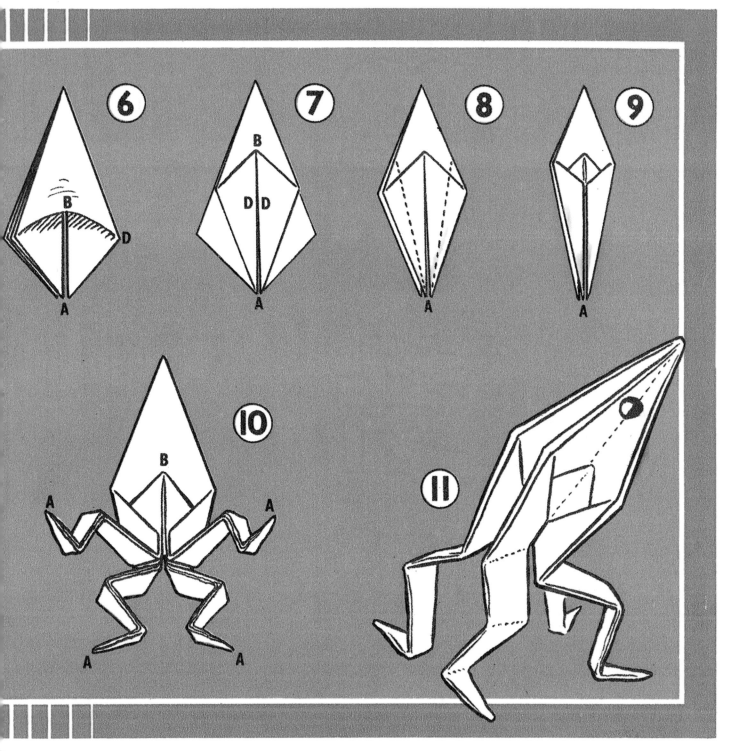

FROG BY FOLDING A SHEET OF PAPER

taking care that B finishes exactly in the middle (Figure 4) and treat the other three points B similarly (Figure 5). Here comes the tricky bit. Put your finger under B and lift (Figure 6), then put the sides AD to the middle line, working the new folds flat until B is pushed to its highest point (Figure 7). It is important to make a neat job of this, so don't hurry it. When all the points B have been treated thus the paper should look like Figure 8. Next fold the lower sides to the middle along the dotted lines to give Figure 9. You now have four narrow points at A. Bring them forward one at a time and crease them as shown in Figure 10. Press the new joints firmly as the "legs" are rather thick. Draw in the eyes if you like and stand the frog up (Figure 11), adjusting the leg creases as necessary to make him balance. With your finger stroke the frog down the middle of his back. As your finger slips off, the frog will jump.

RUPERT'S DIFFERENT CLOTHES

1 RUPERT AND THE LOD INCHEMY	**2** RUPERT AND THE VERRI SECURE	**3** RUPERT AND THE NOWKNUN YEUJORN
4 RUPERT AND THE PROUDGOCH	**5** RUPERT AND THE SLOTWAU	**6** RUPERT'S EPED ESA DAVTUREEN

RUPERT's red jersey and yellow scarf and trousers are so well known that it may surprise you to see him in something else. Here are six costumes he has had in past Annual stories, and underneath are the names of the adventures in which he wore them, but the main words of the titles are jumbled. Can you tell what the funny words ought to be? Then you can guess which costume belongs to each adventure.

Answers on page 68.

Illustrated by JOHN HARROLD

RUPERT's
Birthday
Adventure

Originally published in the *Daily Express*, 2000

John Harrold.

Rupert's Birthday Adventure

RUPERT MEETS COUSIN BEA

When Rupert's birthday comes he sends
Out invitations to his friends ...

"I do hope everybody comes –
I want to play with all my chums!"

As Rupert nears the postbox he
Sees Bill, who's with his cousin Bea ...

"Hello, Bill! This invite's for you –
Please bring your little cousin too."

It is autumn in Nutwood and nearly time for Rupert's birthday. He and Mrs Bear have been planning a special party and are busy writing invitations to all his chums. "I hope I haven't forgotten anybody!" says Rupert. "Check the names on your list," smiles his mother. "There are so many there I think you must have invited the whole class ..." When the final invitation has been written, Rupert sticks stamps on all the envelopes and sets out towards the High Street to post them straightaway.

As Rupert nears the postbox he spots his pal Bill Badger, coming towards him with a new companion ... "Hello!" says Bill. "This is my cousin, Beatrix. She's visiting Nutwood for the first time and will be staying with us for the whole week ... " "Pleased to meet you!" smiles Rupert. "If you're staying all week you'll be able to come to my birthday party too!" "Yes, please!" squeaks the little badger. "Good idea!" smiles Bill. "She's only three but I'm sure she'll enjoy meeting all the others ..."

RUPERT'S PARTY BEGINS

*"At last! It's time!" The guests begin
Arriving. Rupert lets them in …*

*"It's Bea! Come in and join the fun –
You'll soon get to know everyone!"*

*"We'll have a treasure hunt! Look round!
All sorts of prizes to be found …"*

*"Ah, ha!" laughs Bill, then gives a cheer.
"Look, Bea! I think I've found one here."*

For the rest of the week Rupert looks forward excitedly to the day of his party. To everyone's delight the weather stays fine, with autumn sunshine brightening the whole house. "Happy birthday!" cries Tigerlily as Rupert opens the door. "Am I the first one here?" More guests appear and by the time that Bill and Beatrix arrive the room is full of Nutwood pals, all chatting happily. "Hello, you two!" calls Rupert. "Come in and I'll introduce Beatrix to everyone else …"

As it is such a fine, sunny day, Mrs Bear suggests that the chums might like to play in the garden while she prepares their tea. "I've organised a treasure hunt!" she tells them. "There should be enough prizes for everyone, but you'll have to look very carefully to find them all …" Rupert's guests start to search the garden excitedly. "I think I've found something!" calls Willie, reaching under a bush. "And what's this?" laughs Bill. "Look, Beatrix! We've found something too …"

"Look, in the sky!" cries Ottoline.
The others peer at what she's seen.

"It's the Balloonist!" Rupert cries,
A friend the pals all recognise ...

"Hello, I've brought a birthday gift
And come to offer you a lift."

"A flying helmet!" Rupert beams.
He's going for a flight it seems ...

Rupert is still helping his chums search for prizes when he suddenly sees Ottoline, pointing up at the sky ... "Look!" she cries. "A huge balloon!" "It's coming down!" gasps Edward. "I can see the pilot waving." "The Balloonist!" laughs Rupert, recognising his old friend. "He promised he'd come back to Nutwood one day ..." "Hello!" calls the Balloonist as he lands on the lawn. "Hope you don't mind me dropping in like this! I was flying nearby and thought I'd come and wish Rupert a happy birthday!"

As the chums gather round, the Balloonist reaches into his basket and produces a small parcel. "For you!" he tells Rupert. "I hope it's the right size ..." Rupert unwraps the present excitedly. "A flying helmet!" he cries. "How wonderful! It's just like yours ..." "Actually, that's only the first part of the present," the Balloonist tells Mrs Bear. "I really wondered if Rupert fancied a jaunt over Nutwood? Spot of sight-seeing – perhaps just as far as the Professor's tower ..."

RUPERT GETS READY FOR A FLIGHT

"That's just the ticket! We're all set –
I'll hold the basket, in you get …"

"Bea too!" calls Beatrix. "Bea want fly!
In big balloon up in the sky!"

"I don't see why she shouldn't come!
We'll take her and one other chum …"

"We won't be long! A little hop
To see the village, then we'll stop."

Mrs Bear says she's happy for Rupert to go up in the balloon, so long as he doesn't leave the party for too long. "No, no!" laughs the Balloonist. "If we leave straightaway, we'll be back in a jiffy …" Rupert fastens his helmet and gets ready to climb into the basket. "All set!" smiles the Balloonist, then spins round with a cry of surprise. "I say! Who's this?" "Bea!" cries Beatrix. "Bea fly too!" "Oh, dear!" says Bill. "I think she wants to join you …"
The Balloonist picks Beatrix up for a closer look.

"You're a bit small for ballooning!" he laughs. "Still, I don't see why you shouldn't try … your brother could come along too! There's bags of room inside the basket!" Bill is delighted at a chance to join Rupert for an unexpected balloon ride and promises to make sure his cousin is safe and sound. "No need for alarm, Mrs Bear!" says the Balloonist. "We'll simply float gently over Nutwood, then come back down to land where we started …"

Inside the basket, Bea looks round
Then pulls a lever that she's found ...

"Stop!" Rupert calls, but it's too late.
"I say!" the Balloonist gasps. "Wait!"

"Come back!" calls Mrs Bear. "Oh, my!
They're sailing up into the sky ..."

"The lever won't turn back again ...
That means we'll go on climbing then."

Rupert, Bill and Beatrix wait in the basket while the Balloonist says goodbye to Mrs Bear. Bill's cousin is so excited that she keeps jumping up and down, trying to peer over the edge. Before Bill can stop her, she grabs hold of a lever and swings on it with a cry of glee. "Don't!" gasps Rupert. "That works the controls ..." As he speaks, the basket suddenly starts to sway. "What's happening? Help! I say!" cries the Balloonist, tumbling to the ground. "Don't take off without me!"

Rupert and Bill feel the balloon give a sudden lurch, then rise swiftly above the astonished guests. "Come back!" cries Mrs Bear but it is already too late ... the balloon floats higher and higher over the garden until the figures below look tiny. "I can't turn the lever back!" gasps Bill. "It seems to be jammed ..." "Bea flying!" comes a voice from the basket. "At least Beatrix isn't frightened!" says Rupert. "I am!" says Bill. "If we keep on climbing we'll go through the clouds!"

RUPERT FLIES AWAY

The pals keep climbing till they see
Thick cloud all round. "I'm cold!" says Bea.

A sudden strong wind starts to blow –
The pals leave Nutwood far below ...

At last, they wrench the lever free –
"Now we can come down gradually."

The pals descend, to find that they
Must have been carried miles away ...

Sure enough, the balloon keeps climbing until it is completely engulfed in chilly mist. "Brrrr!" shivers Beatrix. "Bea cold!" To the pals' relief, they soon emerge above the clouds, where the sun is shining brightly. "That's better!" laughs Bill. "At least we'll be warm." "We would be if it wasn't so windy!" calls Rupert. "I think we're in for a gale ..." As he speaks a strong gust catches the balloon and sends it speeding through the sky. "Gosh!" blinks Bill. "I'd no idea balloons went so fast!"

Buffeted by the wind, the balloon finally slows to a halt as Rupert wrenches the control lever free. "Well done!" calls Bill. "Now we can try to land ..." Drifting gently down through a thick layer of cloud, the pals peer over the basket at an unfamiliar landscape of trees and rocky hills. "Where are we?" blinks Bill. "I don't know," says Rupert. "We've been blown over Nutwood and beyond the far side of the forest. We must have drifted for miles and miles ..."

RUPERT SEES MORE BALLOONISTS

"Look, there!" Bill gives a startled cry.
"Another balloon in the sky!"

The chums wave to the pilot. "He
Might know which way Nutwood can be ..."

A strong wind blows, the chums fly on,
It seems their only hope has gone!

Then, suddenly, the pals see more
Balloons. "Where are they heading for?"

To Bill's astonishment, he suddenly spots another balloon, floating nearby. "Look!" he cries. "It's coming towards us!" As the balloon gets closer, the chums wave to attract the pilot's attention. "He'll be able to tell us where we are!" says Rupert. "With a bit of luck he might know the way back to Nutwood ..." "Hello!" calls Bill. "I wonder if you can help us?" "I say!" gasps Rupert. "The Balloonist!" "That's who I'm calling to!" says Bill. "No, our Balloonist!" says Rupert. "The pilot looks just like him!"

The pilot of the second balloon turns to the pals and waves but, before he can say anything, a sudden gust of wind sends them racing on ahead. "We'll just have to hope he catches up soon!" shrugs Bill. "He must have borrowed another balloon and come all the way from Nutwood to look for us ..." As the chums glance back, they are amazed to see more balloons appear – all flying in the same direction. "I don't understand!" blinks Rupert. "I wonder if he's organised a search party?"

RUPERT GAINS AN ESCORT

*Two storks appear. "A splendid race –
You've really set a cracking pace!"*

*"Don't slow down now! You're in the lead –
Just keep on flying at full speed!"*

*The pals continue on their flight –
A great castle comes into sight …*

*The pair of storks swoop down to land
Where birds of every kind all stand.*

Rupert and Bill are still staring at the cluster of balloons when a sudden cry makes them spin round in surprise. Two enormous storks hover nearby, beating the air with their wings. "Ahoy there!" cries the first bird. "You're the first balloon we've seen!" "Hello!" stammers Rupert. "I wonder if you can tell us the way back to Nutwood?" "Back?" squawks the bird incredulously. "You don't want to go back! You're in the lead! I don't think any of the others will catch up with you now …"

As the storks fly on ahead, Rupert and Bill realise that they have accidentally entered a giant balloon race … "And we're in the lead!" marvels Bill. The next minute the pals spot a far-off castle, perched high on one of the rocky peaks. "Look, Bill!" cries Rupert. "It's surrounded by birds! Just like the Bird King's Palace …" As they near the castle the pair see the storks swoop gracefully down to greet a court official. "The end of the race!" gasps Rupert. "I think we're meant to land there too!"

RUPERT AND HIS CHUMS LAND

"Our journey's over!" Rupert calls.
The balloon stops, then slowly falls …

"Bravo!" the birds call, flocking round
As the basket lands on the ground.

"Well done! A splendid victory!
It will delight His Majesty …"

"The King approves of balloons! They're
The quietest manned craft in the air!"

Rupert pulls sharply at the balloon's controls as they hover over the terrace. "Bea landing!" calls Beatrix as the basket starts to fall. "Not too fast!" warns Bill but by lifting the lever gradually, Rupert manages to touch down with only a gentle bump. "Bravo!" cry the excited birds. "Three cheers for the winners!" "I say!" blinks Rupert. "That's the Bird King's Chamberlain. I wonder if the King is here too? He doesn't normally approve of anyone flying, except for birds …"

To Rupert's surprise, the Chamberlain seems delighted and hurries forward to offer his congratulations … "Well done!" he smiles. "A memorable victory. His Majesty will be pleased!" "Thank you," blinks Rupert. "But I thought the King didn't like people flying …" "That's because he hates noisy machines," explains the courtier. "Balloons are different. Silent, graceful, skilfully flown. His Majesty runs an annual balloon race in the hope of encouraging more pilots to take it up …"

"It's the Balloonist!" Rupert blinks.
"He must have followed us!" he thinks.

A trumpet blows. The King appears.
"A wonderful result!" he cheers.

The Bird King meets the winning crew –
"My goodness! Rupert Bear! It's you ..."

"Well done!" another pilot beams.
"You left us all behind, it seems ..."

As more birds gather round to see the winners, Rupert spots a fleet of other balloonists, gliding gently down to join them ... "There's our chum!" he cries. "I hope he won't mind us stealing his prize! First we make off in his balloon, then a sudden gust of wind puts us out in the lead ..." To the pals' relief, the Balloonist doesn't seem at all put out at being runner up. He waves back to Rupert but before they can speak a trumpeter announces the Bird King's arrival ...

The Bird King takes a gleaming cup and prepares to present it to the winning crew ... "Rupert!" he blinks. "Young Rupert Bear, from Nutwood, I didn't know you went ballooning ..." "I don't! I mean, I haven't, very often," says Rupert. "This is the first race Bill and I have ever entered ..." "Beginners' luck, then!" laughs the King. "Still, you won the trophy, fair and square!" "Quite right!" calls another balloonist. "First rate flying! Saw it all as I followed you here ..."

Next moment, the Balloonist comes –
"Bravo!" he cries and greets the chums.

"I'll just jot down your names! Please tell
Me yours first, then your friends' as well …"

"We met this morning! When you flew
To Nutwood! You met Bill there too …"

"Nutwood? I recognise the name,
But I've not been there, all the same …"

As the other competitors gather round to congratulate Rupert and Bill, their friend, the Balloonist, comes hurrying over to join them. "Bravo!" he smiles. "Thought I'd almost caught up there, then that last minute dash left me standing …" To the chums' surprise, he makes no mention of the mishap that sent them on their way but takes out a notebook and asks Rupert to spell his name. "For the Ballooning Gazette!" he laughs. "They always like a detailed report of who won …"

The two chums are astonished by the Balloonist's question … "You already know who I am!" blinks Rupert. "This is my friend, Bill Badger and his cousin, Beatrix. We'd never have been on a balloon ride if you hadn't landed in Nutwood and come to visit my party …" As Rupert speaks, it is the Balloonist's turn to look mystified … "Nutwood?" he murmurs. "Nut as in hazel and wood as in tree? It sounds familiar, but I don't think I've ever been there. There must be some mistake …"

RUPERT SOLVES THE MYSTERY

*"We flew away in your balloon!
You can't have forgotten so soon …"*

*"My brother, Hector! He must be
The one you mean. Looks just like me."*

*"You're Rupert Bear! My brother's friend –
I'm glad the mystery's at an end!"*

*"The balloon race was fun but how
Can we get back to Nutwood now?"*

Rupert is dumbfounded. "You can't have forgotten everything that happened …" he protests. "You visited Nutwood earlier today and gave Bill and me a ride in your balloon! That's how we came to join the race …" "My balloon?" blinks the pilot, then he suddenly smiles. "Of course! I know what's caused the confusion. This isn't mine. It belongs to my brother, Hector! We're both balloonists, you see. He's the one who told me about Nutwood. Got a friend there called Rudolph, I think …"

"That's me!" laughs Rupert. "Only my name's not Rudolph! I met your brother when his balloon came down on Nutwood Common. I didn't know there were two of you …" "We're twins!" explains the stranger. "My name's Horace!" Rupert explains how the chums came to be cast adrift in the balloon. "Astonishing!" he blinks. "And you went on to win the race …" "That's all very well," says Rupert. "But what we really want to do is get back to Nutwood. Everyone will be terribly worried if we're not home soon!"

RUPERT DEPARTS

"The only way to travel back
Is wait till the wind changes tack!"

A marshal waves a flag to show
The wind has changed. It's time to go …

"Stand by to cast off! In you hop –
We'll fly to Nutwood now, non-stop …"

The Bird King waves and calls "Goodbye!"
As the balloons take to the sky.

When the Bird King hears how Rupert and Bill are keen to get back to Nutwood, he shakes his head and shrugs. "That's the only drawback to balloons, I'm afraid. They can only travel in the same direction as the wind! You'll have to wait until it changes …" "But that could take ages!" groans Bill. "We might be here for days!" As he speaks, a marshal appears with a brightly coloured flag. "Attention all balloonists!" he calls. "The wind is turning, from East to West!"

"Time you were off!" declares Horace. He helps Rupert and Bill clamber into their basket then lifts Beatrix gently over the side. "A Westerly wind should be perfect!" he smiles. "You'll be back in Nutwood in no time at all …" laughs Horace. "What if we miss it?" asks Bill. "Don't worry!" laughs Horace. "I'm sure it's on my map …" "Your map?" asks Rupert. "Yes!" beams Horace. "I've decided to come too!" "Goodbye!" calls the Bird King as the balloons take off. "Congratulations on winning the race!"

RUPERT RETURNS TO NUTWOOD

The chums keep Horace well in sight –
"Straight on!" he calls. "The wind's just right!"

At last! A sight the chums both know –
"It's Nutwood! Almost straight below ..."

"I'll pull the lever slowly, then
We should go safely down again."

In Rupert's garden, all his friends
Call out as the balloon flight ends ...

The two balloons are soon carried off by a stiff Westerly breeze, leaving the Bird King and his Court officials far behind ... "I wonder if we're still going in the right direction?" says Bill. "I can't see any landmarks I recognise ..." As if to answer his question, Horace looks up from his map reading and points excitedly ahead ... "Nutwood!" cries Rupert. "Look, Bill. I can see the church tower and all the houses of the village. It won't be long before we're right overhead!"

Rupert waits until the balloon is directly above his garden, then pulls the control lever to send it gently down ... "Bea back!" cries Beatrix happily. "Yes!" smiles Bill. "Just wait till all the others hear where we've been ..." As the balloon comes down to land, Rupert spots his chums all peering up excitedly. "Well done!" calls the old Professor. "I saw you approaching through my telescope. It's lucky the wind changed directions or who knows where you would have landed?"

"Thank goodness!" Mrs Bear cries. "We
Had no idea where you could be!"

"All's well that ends well!" Horace cries.
"These youngsters even won a prize!"

"Congratulations, Mrs Bear!
Your son's team beat us, fair and square!"

Then Rupert sees that Bea has stayed
Behind. "What's wrong? She looks dismayed ..."

The balloon lands perfectly and Rupert is soon telling his mother all about the unexpected journey and how he and Bill won a special race. "Thank goodness you're back safely!" declares Mrs Bear. "The Professor was all ready to go and look for you in one of his flying machines!" "No need, by the look of things!" smiles Hector. "But tell me more about the race. The Bird King's Cup is a trophy I've always wanted to win ..." "Me too!" calls Horace as he glides to join the others ...

Hector is delighted to see his brother and soon introduces him to all the party guests. "We're both keen balloonists," he tells Mrs Bear. "Capital sport!" nods Horace. "Particularly when it brings you to such charming places ..." Hector insists on hearing how the pals followed the marshals to the Bird King's palace. "We didn't even know it was a race!" says Bill. Rupert is just about to join them when he notices Beatrix, peering fearfully out from behind a basket ...

RUPERT GETS A BIRTHDAY CAKE

"Don't worry!" Rupert laughs. "I'm sure
That he won't be cross any more ..."

"An accident!" smiles Hector. "You
Know, I once did the same thing too!"

As Hector hears of Rupert's ride
He carries little Bea inside ...

"Three cheers for Rupert, Bill and Bea!"
Says Rupert's mother. "Time for tea!"

Rupert kneels down to talk to Bill's cousin. "Whatever's the matter?" he asks. "Loonist cross!" she sniffs. "Bea make loon fly ..." "Don't worry!" smiles Rupert. "Hector won't be cross. He knows you didn't mean to make the balloon go without him ..." "Rather!" smiles the Balloonist, hoisting Beatrix up for a chat. "All an accident. It could have happened to anyone! Once did the same thing myself, come to think of it. Up in the clouds before I knew what was happening ..."

Hector carries Beatrix indoors to join the rest of the party guests. "I'm jolly glad to see you all back safe and sound!" he says. "Winning that cup was a stroke of good fortune too! Horace and I have been after it for ages ..." "Richly deserved!" beams his brother. "First-rate flying! Rupert, Bill and Beatrix must be the youngest champions ever!" "Happy birthday, dear!" says Mrs Bear as she brings in Rupert's cake. "You certainly seem to have had an exciting party!"

THE
END

51

HOW TO MAKE RUPERT'S BOAT (1)

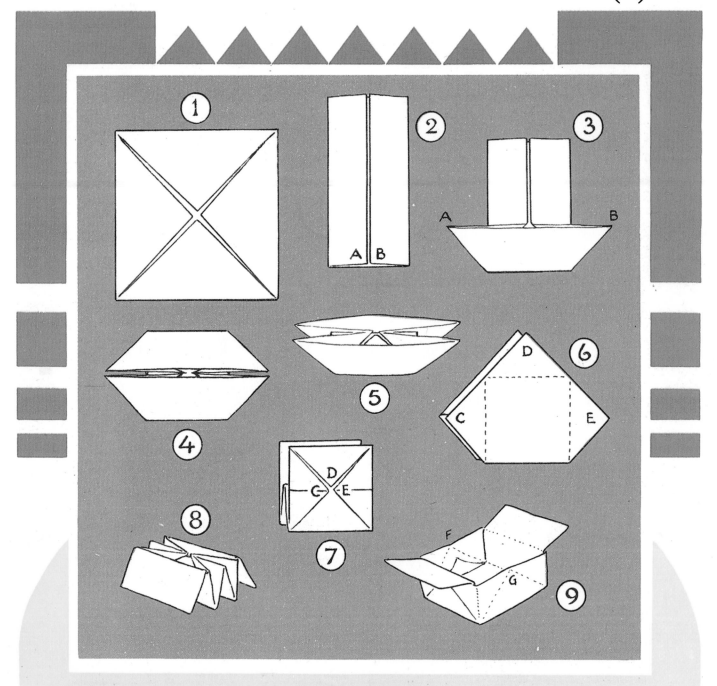

THIS trick is very old and is said to have come from China.

Take a fair-sized square of paper and fold the four corners to the middle to make Figure 1. Next turn the top and bottom sides to the middle, press the folds firmly, then open them out and turn the other sides to the middle to make Figure 2. Now pinch the corners A and B and lift them outwards and upwards to bring the bottom edge up to the middle (Figure 3). Do the same with the top corners to make Figure 4. Press all folds firmly again and fold the shape in half as in Figure 5 which looks like two little canoes side by side. Inside each "canoe" is a loose piece of paper. Pull these out (Figure 6) and fold the corners C, D and E along the dotted lines. Repeat with the other side and you have Figure 7. Now fold down the top half of each side to make Figure 8 which looks like a small purse, and if you take the two flaps, pull them slightly apart and

HOW TO MAKE RUPERT'S BOAT (2)

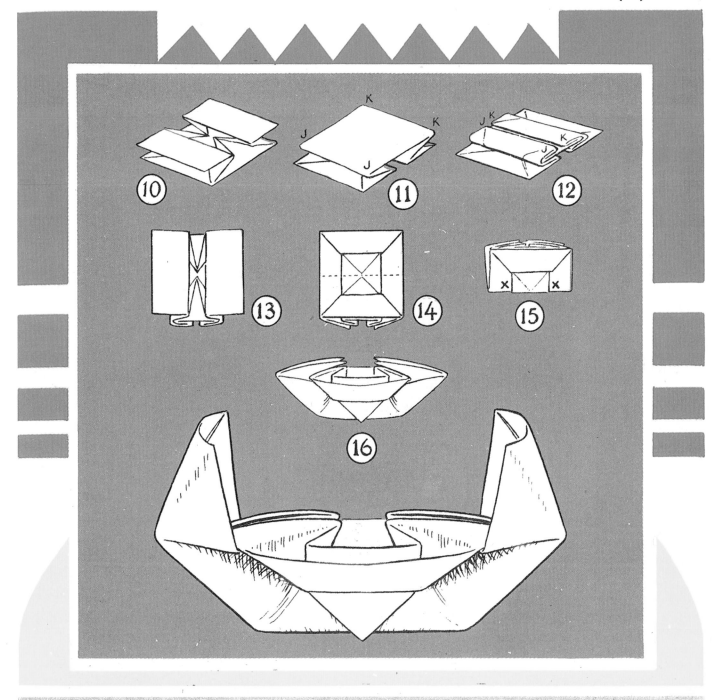

push the middle down you will get a box (Figure 9). Push the points F and G down so that they meet at the bottom of the box and the flaps come together (Figure 10), turn the thing over (Figure 11) and fold the sides JJ and KK to the middle as in Figure 12. (These last folds will be rather tough as there are several thicknesses of paper there.) Next turn the whole thing over and it should look like Figure 13. Pull the flaps slightly apart and you will see the points F and G still nestling there. Pull the flaps more firmly and let them go round to the back of the figure, at the same time working F and G to the upper and lower edges to make Figure 14. Fold this in half along the dotted line (Figure 15), take hold exactly at the places marked XX and pull firmly outwards and upwards (but without jerking) and the boat will appear rather unexpectedly. Finally our old friends, the flaps, can be raised to make the "sails" and the trick is done.

RUPERT'S PICTURE PUZZLE

This picture was painted by Alex Cubie for Rupert's Adventure Series. It shows Rupert and his mummy playing a game which you can join in too.

Every letter in the alphabet is represented by at least one of the objects in this room. Can you write down what they all are?

Answers on page 68.

HOW TO MAKE
A CHRISTMAS TREE

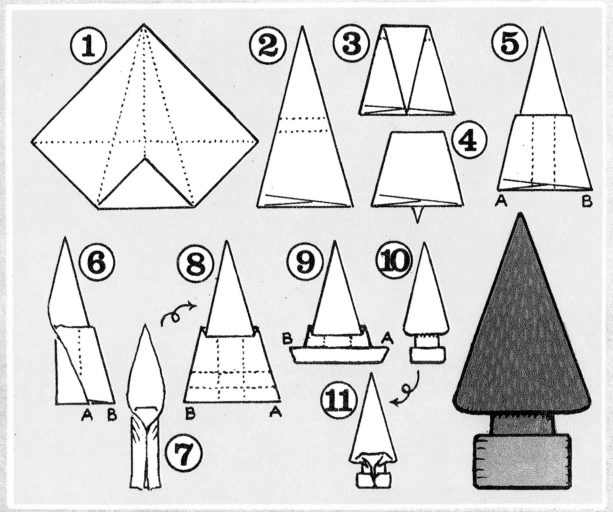

You can make a Christmas tree with a square of thin paper. Fold opposite corners together each way to find the middle and fold one corner part way to the centre (Figure 1). Fold both sides in along the sloping dotted lined (Figure 2), note the new dotted lines and bring the top point to the middle of the bottom edge to give the upper crease (Figure 3) and then fold the point backwards using the other dotted line (Figure 4). Bring the point up again keeping both folds pressed (Figure 5) and mark two upright lines, as shown, at equal distances from the corners A and B. Take A across to a spot on the bottom edge that will make a fold at the lefthand dotted line. Press that fold

only as far up as the middle crease (Figure 6) and do the same to B so that A and B can be held forward together (Figure 7). Separate A and B as in Figure 5 and turn the paper over (Figure 8). Fold the bottom edge up, then over again following the horizontal dotted lines (Figure 9). Take B and A round to the back and the creases of Figure 6 and 7 will cause the Christmas tree (Figure 10) to take shape. Turn it over again (Figure 11), lock the end of B into A, then gently flatten the folds at the back into the form required. If the 'tub' is slightly rounded the tree will stand up.

(*This version of his Christmas tree was sent to Rupert by Mr Robert Harbin, the Origami man.*)

55

Rupert and the Snowbird

Illustrated by STUART TROTTER

RUPERT
and the
Snowbird

RUPERT RECEIVES A PARCEL

One morning, Rupert cannot wait
To greet the postman at the gate!

"Here's Mummy's catalogue at last!"
Cheers Rupert, as he dashes past.

This book from the department store
Is full of Christmas gifts galore.

Says Rupert, "Choosing toys is fun!"
He lists his choices one by one.

It is a chilly winter day, and Rupert has been waiting all morning for the postman to arrive.

"Good morning, Rupert!" the postman beams, as Rupert greets him at the gate of the Bears' cottage. "I have a parcel for your mum here."

"Hurrah, it's here at last!" Rupert cheers. "Thank you!" The little bear runs back inside with the parcel, dashing past his father in his haste.

"What's the hurry?" Mr Bear chuckles.

"Mummy's catalogue from the department store has arrived!" says Rupert breathlessly. He rushes into the living room to find his mum, and climbs onto her lap.

"The catalogue's come just in time," says Mrs Bear to Rupert with a smile, as they pore over the book. "Now you can write your Christmas list! I'm sure you'll have no trouble finding things you'd like."

"It's so much fun choosing toys," sighs Rupert, and he sets to writing his list. "First, I'd like this racing car ... "

RUPERT GOES TO NUTCHESTER

As Rupert trims the Christmas tree,
Mum asks, "Please come to town with me."

So off to Nutchester they go,
Although the grey sky hints at snow.

"Mum, look!" cries Rupert in delight;
The town is such a festive sight!

Bright Christmas decorations draw
The people to this lavish store.

Christmas is but a few days away, and Rupert is growing more and more excited. Dad has found the perfect Christmas tree for the cottage, and he asks Rupert to help him trim it.

But Mum also has a special favour to ask of Rupert: "Please would you come to town with me? I still have some Christmas presents to buy."

So Rupert and Mum wrap up warm in scarves and overcoats, and catch the busy bus to Nutchester.

As they drive to town, the sky turns grey. "It looks as if it might snow," says Mum. "Let's hope we get back before it starts!"

But Mum's worries are forgotten as she and Rupert arrive in Nutchester. The town is bedecked in festive twinkling lights, and a brass band plays carols in the town square. The people passing the department store are drawn to the beautiful Christmas tree in the window, draped in ornaments.

RUPERT AND BILL SEE SANTA

"Hi, Bill!" calls Rupert to his chum,
Who's busy shopping with his mum.

The friends are anxious to explore
The toy department of the store.

Their pals from school are all here, too,
And waiting in a lengthy queue.

"Oh, look!" says Rupert, "Santa's here!
Let's tell him what we'd like this year."

As Rupert steps through the door of the store he sees somebody he knows well. "Hi, Bill!" he calls to his chum, who is helping his mum with the Christmas shopping too.

Mrs Bear and Mrs Badger tell the friends they may look around the toy department while they shop for groceries. Rupert and Bill ride the escalator to the bustling toy department, and gasp in delight as they step inside. On every shelf there are toys and games: sailing boats, footballs, jigsaws and rocking-horses!

Rupert spots more of his schoolfriends among the crowds. "There's Edward Trunk, Algy Pug and Podgy Pig!" cries Rupert. "They're in an awfully long queue. I wonder what they're waiting for?"

Rupert and Bill join the line behind their chums, and as it moves forward Rupert sees what all the excitement and busy-ness is about!

"Oh, look, Bill," Rupert exclaims, "Santa Claus is here! Let's give him our Christmas lists, shall we?"

THE BUS STRUGGLES IN THE SNOW

But Mum appears and says, "Let's go!
Outside it's just begun to snow."

The two friends do not make a fuss,
And board the busy Nutwood bus.

The storm grows worse, snow all around;
The bus skids on the icy ground.

Then as it struggles up a rise,
Its wheels get stuck. The engine dies!

But as Rupert and Bill near the front of the queue, their mothers slip through the crowds towards them with their arms full of parcels.

"I'm afraid we need to leave right away," says Mrs Bear. "It's just begun to snow outside and if we wait any longer we may not be able to get home!"

Rupert and Bill are secretly disappointed not to have had the chance to give Santa their Christmas lists, but they know Mrs Bear is right.

Outside the snow is already falling heavily as Rupert and Bill board the Nutwood bus. It is nearly full and Rupert and Bill must share a seat.

The bus pulls out of Nutchester. But before very long it runs into trouble, skidding on the icy lanes and buffeting against the snowy banks. Suddenly, as the driver steers the bus up the hill, the wheels jam and, with a sorry sputter, the engine gives out.

The bus is well and truly stuck!

RUPERT AND BILL GO FOR HELP

"Don't worry, Mum," says Rupert Bear,
"We'll go for help. You stay right there."

So through the snow the chums both trudge,
To tell someone their bus won't budge.

"They'll be all right," Bill Badger sighs,
As overhead a shadow flies.

Then poor old Rupert stubs his toe –
He's tripped on something in the snow!

"Oh dear!" sighs Mrs Bear. "It looks like we might be here for a while."

Rupert peers out of the window. The snow is still falling steadily, but he can just make out the lights of Nutchester. "Don't worry, Mum," says Rupert. "Bill and I will walk back to town and fetch help. You stay here. We shan't be long."

Rupert and his chum climb off the bus and begin to trudge through the snow, which is waist-deep in parts.

They stop by a tree and glance back at the bus.

"I hope everyone will be all right while we're gone," sighs Bill, worriedly, trying to catch a glimpse of his mum.

Neither friend sees a large shadow swooping overhead!

"We should hurry, though," says Rupert. "It's getting dark already." He ploughs on ... but suddenly the toe of his boot hits something buried beneath the snow, and he trips over.

"Ouch!" he yelps.

RUPERT DISCOVERS AN EGG

*"A giant egg! How can that be?
Most eggs are laid in spring," says he.*

*He holds it up most carefully.
"I wonder whose egg this can be?"*

*A Snowbird lands nearby and caws,
"It's mine! It just slipped from my claws!"*

*"I'm in your debt!" exclaims the bird.
"I'll fly you home – just say the word."*

Rupert scrambles to his hands and knees and sweeps away the snow that covers the thing he has tripped over.

"A giant egg? How can that be?" he wonders. "I can't think of any bird that lays its eggs in winter, only in spring!"

Rupert lifts the egg with great care. It feels light, yet solid. "I wonder whose egg this can be?" he frowns.

Suddenly, a large, glossy white bird swoops down from the sky and perches nearby.

"Thank goodness! You found my egg! I was keeping it safe from the storm, and it slipped from my claws," she caws sadly.

"It's a very strong egg," says Rupert in awe. "Please, what sort of bird are you?"

"I am a Snowbird," she explains. "We only lay our eggs when it snows. Please tell me how I can thank you for looking after my egg. May I fly you home?"

Bill, who is terribly cold now, is about to say *yes, please*.

RUPERT AND BILL ASK FOR HELP

"Our bus is stranded in the snow –
Without some help it just won't go!"

Upon the Snowbird's back they climb
And hope they'll reach the town in time.

But wait! The Snowbird's flown too far!
Soon Rupert can't tell where they are.

They see a castle up ahead
And there the Snowbird flies instead!

But Rupert reminds his friend of the bus passengers who are waiting to be rescued. "Our bus broke down and we need to fetch help," Rupert tells the Snowbird. "Could you fly us back to Nutchester, please?"

The Snowbird is glad to do this favour for the friends. She invites Rupert and Bill to climb upon her back, and they nestle gladly among her soft feathers. Rupert keeps careful hold of the precious egg as the Snowbird takes off and flies through the snowy sky.

As Rupert peers over Bill's shoulder to look for the lights of Nutchester, he notices that the town is already far behind, and the scenery below is unfamiliar. The Snowbird has flown too far!

"Please!" Rupert cries. "This isn't Nutchester! We need to turn back. Everyone on the bus will be wondering where we've got to."

But the Snowbird does not answer. She soars above the clouds and on towards a magnificent castle!

RUPERT TELLS SANTA THE STORY

The Snowbird lands upon the wall
And Santa comes to greet them all!

When Rupert tells him of their plight,
Dear Santa plans a rescue flight.

At once the elves prepare the sleigh
So Santa can be on his way.

Then through the chilly winter sky,
Down to the bus, the friends now fly.

As the Snowbird lands gracefully on the castle wall, Rupert forgets his worries and gives a delighted cheer as Santa Claus comes to greet them.

"My dear friend Snowbird! You've brought young Rupert and Bill to visit me!" Santa beams.

"We need your help, please, Santa," caws the Snowbird. Rupert tells Santa the whole story of how the bus broke down in the snow and how he happened upon the Snowbird's egg.

"We must rescue the people on the bus," Santa declares. "Let's fly the sleigh down right away."

Santa's elves have been loading the sleigh ready for Christmas Eve, but now they empty it to make room for Rupert and Bill. The two chums help unload all the beautifully-wrapped gifts, then they settle in the cosy sleigh as Santa takes up the reins. With the Snowbird following close by, the sleigh flies to the rescue.

But first it must make a special stop ...

SANTA HELPS RUPERT AND THE SNOWBIRD

And as they pass the Snowbird's nest
The egg's returned; now she can rest.

She waves her new friends on their way:
"I'll see you both again one day!"

The passengers can't wait to climb
Aboard the sleigh; it's just in time!

"Now, Rupert," Santa says, "I see
That you have something there for me!"

The sleigh passes by a strange cloud that shimmers brightly among the dark grey snow clouds, and Rupert realises that this is the Snowbird's nest. Santa lays the Snowbird's egg within the billows of the cloud, and the Snowbird rests upon it. "The egg will hatch soon," says Santa, "but until then she must take good care of it."

"Thank you, Rupert," the Snowbird sings in a lilting, chirruping voice that sounds different from her worried cawing song. "I hope I'll see you again soon."

"Thank you for your help, Snowbird," Rupert says with a wave.

Mrs Bear and Mrs Badger are amazed to see the sleigh swoop down and come to a halt near the stricken bus. Rupert and Bill hop out to let the delighted passengers climb into the sleigh, safe and warm at last.

"Now, Rupert," says Santa with a kindly smile to the tired little bear, "I believe you had something to give me earlier. May I have your Christmas list?"

RUPERT HAS A WONDERFUL SURPRISE

Poor Daddy can't believe his eyes!
"That's not the Nutwood bus!" he cries.

On Christmas Day, something's amiss
In Rupert's stocking: "Why, what's this?"

He blows the whistle loud and long –
It sounds just like … the Snowbird's song!

To Rupert's great delight, it brings
Two pairs of snow-white feathered wings!

Poor Mr Bear has been terribly worried as Mrs Bear and Rupert are so late home from Nutchester. But his worry turns to astonishment as Santa's sleigh flies towards the Bears' cottage, with both of them on board!

On Christmas Day, Rupert finds a stocking at the foot of his bed from his dear friend Santa! Rupert reaches inside the stocking and pulls out a small, golden object.

"It looks like a whistle," says Dad, when Rupert asks him what it might be.

When Rupert blows into it, it makes a lilting, chirruping tune that sounds very familiar.

"That's the Snowbird's song!" Rupert declares. "But what –?" He is interrupted by a gentle tapping at the window. There, outside, he sees the Snowbird, summoned by the whistle, with her glossy white wing wrapped around her brand-new chick!

Rupert is delighted to see the Snowbird's baby. "That's the best Christmas present of all!" he exclaims.

RUPERT'S MEMORY TEST

Now you have read the whole book, have a go at Rupert's
Memory Test. Each of these pictures appears in one of the stories.
Look carefully at the pictures, then try to answer the questions!

1 What are Rupert, Bill and Edward making?

2 Who is the culprit?

3 Rupert and his friends are playing what?

4 Who is coming towards Rupert and Bill?

5 What is strange about the tree?

6 What is the kitten doing?

7 What has Mrs Bear organised for Rupert's party?

8 Who has fallen out of the balloon?

9 Who awards Rupert the cup?

10 Rupert is on the bus to where?

11 What has Rupert tripped over?

12 Who greets the Snowbird?

ANSWERS TO PUZZLES

P15, RUPERT'S SHORT CUT

Algy finds the short cut.

P34, RUPERT'S DIFFERENT CLOTHES

A4—RUPERT AND THE COUGHDROP
B5—RUPERT AND THE OUTLAWS
C6—RUPERT'S DEEP SEA ADVENTURE
D1—RUPERT AND THE OLD CHIMNEY
E2—RUPERT AND THE RIVER RESCUE
F3—RUPERT AND THE UNKNOWN
JOURNEY

P54, RUPERT'S PICTURE PUZZLE

A – Arrows, B – Basin, C – Chair, D – Desk, E – Engine, F – Fan, G – Gun, H – Hat, I – Ink, J – Jug, K – Kettle, L – Lamp, M – Mirror, N – Net, O – Orange, P – Pan, Q – Quiver, R – Radio, S – Sword, T – Top, U – Umbrella, V – Vase, W – Watch, X – On building brick, Y – Yacht, Z – Zebra. See how many others you can find.

P67, RUPERT'S MEMORY TEST

1. snowballs, 2. Wally Wolf, 3. football, 4. Tigerlily, 5. its roots are in the air; it is upside-down, 6. flying, 7. a treasure hunt, 8. the Balloonist, 9. the Bird King, 10. Nutchester, 11. the Snowbird's egg, 12. Santa.

CELEBRATING
90
1920 - 2010

HAPPY 90TH BIRTHDAY,
RUPERT BEAR™

To celebrate, Egmont is publishing two fantastic books which would make perfect gifts:

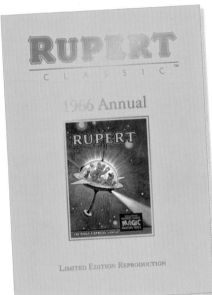

Rupert Bear Annual 1966 (Facsimile)

978 1 4052 5352 9 / £25
Publishing 4th October 2010

This is a limited edition reproduction of the 1966 Rupert Bear Annual, presented in a slipcase together with a certificate of authenticity. Only 3,500 copies will be printed and each will be individually numbered, making them unique and highly collectable.

The Rupert Companion:
A complete history of Rupert Bear, written by Ian Robinson

978 1 4052 5330 7 / £25
Publishing 1st November 2010

This beautiful hardback book begins with Rupert Bear's first appearance in the *Daily Express* and charts his journey to the present day, paying particular attention to the writers and artists who have brought him to life over the years.

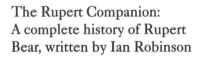

A must for all Rupert Bear fans!

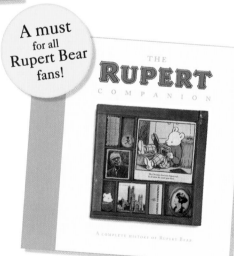

For £5.00* off please order through www.egmont.co.uk

All prices and specifications are correct at time of going to press, however all are subject to change. *Offer will be available for 2 months after publication date of each title.

EGMONT